THIS CANDLEWICK BOOK BELONGS TO:

_____

_____

_____

_____

For Hannah,
all-by-herself
M. W.

For Georgie,
and Eddie Huntley
P. B.

Text copyright © 1992 by Martin Waddell
Illustrations copyright © 1992 by Patrick Benson

First U.S. paperback edition 2002

The Library of Congress has cataloged the hardcover
edition as follows:

Waddell, Martin.
Owl babies / by Martin Waddell ; illustrated by
Patrick Benson.
Summary: Three owl babies whose mother has gone
out in the night try to stay calm while she is gone.
ISBN 978-1-56402-101-4 (hardcover)
[1. Owls — Fiction. 2. Mother and child — Fiction.]
I. Benson, Patrick, ill. II. Title.
PZ7.W1137Ow 1992
[E] — dc20   91-58750

ISBN 978-0-7636-1283-2 (big book)

ISBN 978-1-56402-965-2 (board book)

ISBN 978-0-7636-1710-3 (paperback)

20 19 18

Printed in China

The book was typeset in Caslon Antique.
The illustrations were done with black ink and
watercolor crosshatching.

Candlewick Press
99 Dover Street
Somerville, Massachusetts 02144

visit us at www.candlewick.com

OWL BABIES

Written by
Martin Waddell

Illustrated by
Patrick Benson

CANDLEWICK PRESS

Once there were three baby owls:
Sarah and Percy and Bill.
They lived in a hole
in the trunk of a tree
with their Owl Mother.
The hole had twigs and
leaves and owl feathers in it.
It was their house.

One night they woke up and
their Owl Mother was GONE.
"Where's Mommy?" asked Sarah.
"Oh my goodness!" said Percy.
"I want my mommy!" said Bill.

The baby owls *thought*
(all owls think a lot) –
"I think she's gone hunting," said Sarah.
"To get us our food!" said Percy.
"I want my mommy!" said Bill.

But their Owl Mother didn't come.
The baby owls came out of
their house, and they sat
on the tree and waited.

A big branch for Sarah,
a small branch for Percy,
and an old piece of ivy for Bill.
"She'll be back," said Sarah.
"Back *soon*!" said Percy.
"I want my mommy!" said Bill.

It was dark in the woods and they had to be brave, for things *moved* all around them.

"She'll bring us mice and things that are nice," said Sarah.

"I suppose so!" said Percy.

"I want my mommy!" said Bill.

They sat and they thought
(all owls think a lot) –
"I think we should *all*
sit on *my* branch," said Sarah.
And they did,
all three together.

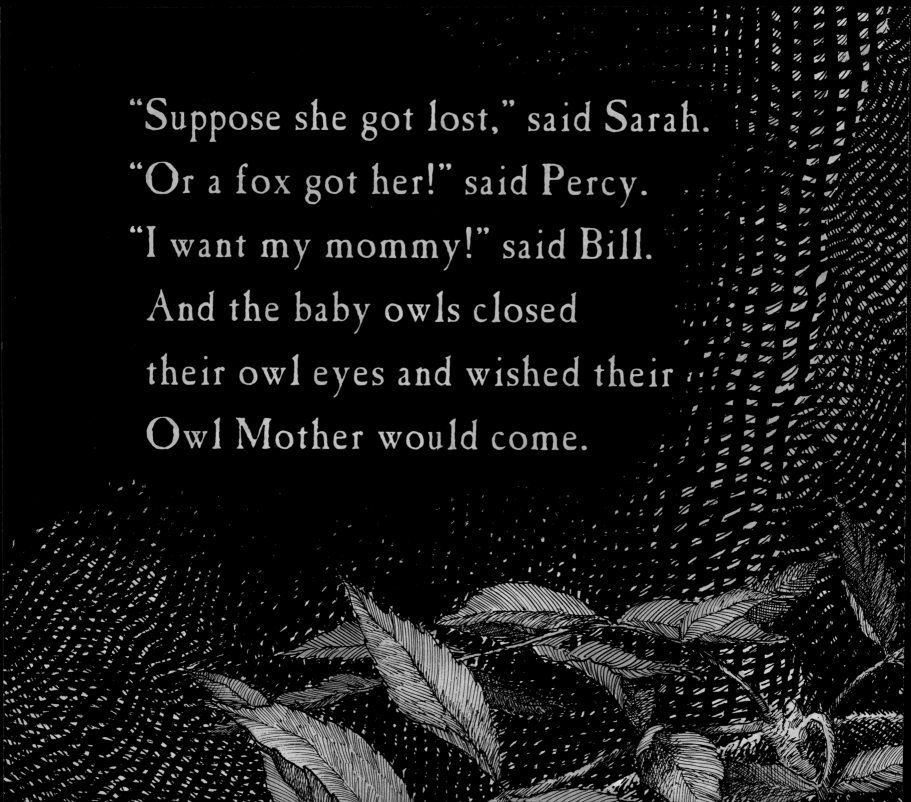

"Suppose she got lost," said Sarah.

"Or a fox got her!" said Percy.

"I want my mommy!" said Bill.

And the baby owls closed
their owl eyes and wished their
Owl Mother would come.

AND SHE CAME.

Soft and silent, she swooped
through the trees
to Sarah and Percy
and Bill.

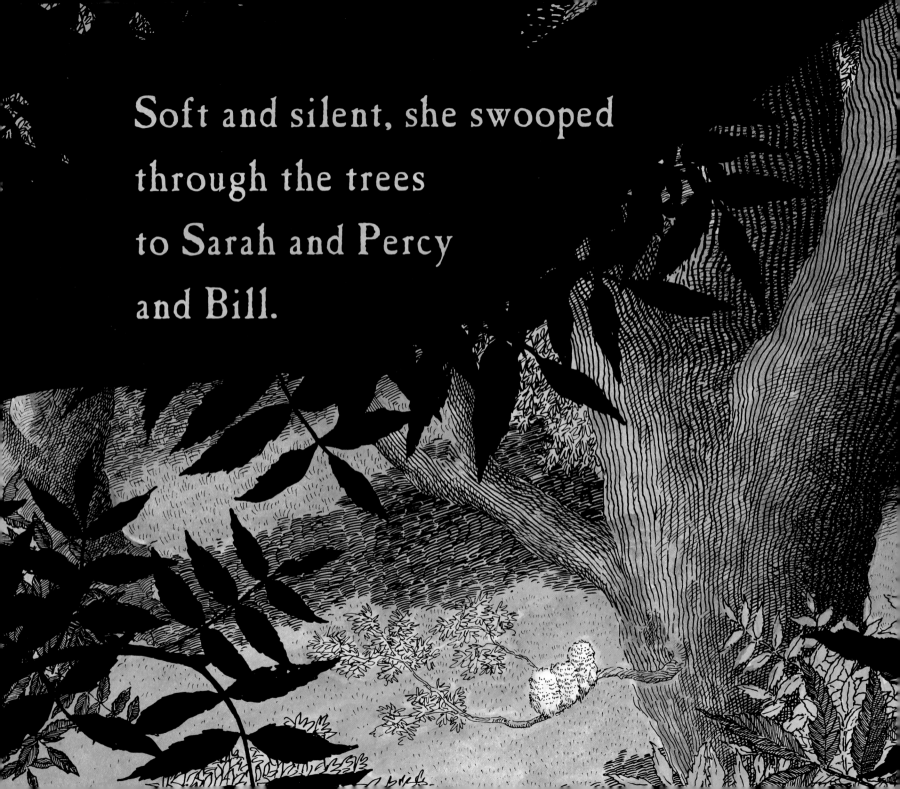

"Mommy!" they cried,
and they flapped and they danced,
and they bounced up and down
on their branch.

"WHAT'S ALL THE FUSS?"
their Owl Mother asked.
"You knew I'd come back."
The baby owls thought
(all owls think a lot) –
"I knew it," said Sarah.
"And I knew it!" said Percy.
"I love my mommy!" said Bill.

MARTIN WADDELL was inspired to write *Owl Babies* after a trip to the market, where he had encountered a lost child ceaselessly wailing, "I want my mommy!" He is the author of more than 100 books for children and young adults. His much-loved picture books include the bestsellers *Farmer Duck, A Kitten Called Moonlight, The Pig in the Pond, Tom Rabbit,* and the Little Bear books. He believes that a picture book's theme should relate directly to events and experiences in a young child's life. "Because emotion is a child's driving force," he says, "each of my picture books is about a very big emotion—like loneliness, fear of the dark, or compassion—in a very small person." Martin Waddell and his wife live in Northern Ireland.

PATRICK BENSON, who usually works using a crosshatch technique, wanted "a more graphic image—rather like a woodcut" for this book and decided to use a blown-up version of his crosshatching. He is the illustrator of many picture books, including *A Christmas Carol, The Little Boat, The Lord Fish, The Sea-Thing Child,* and *Squeak's Good Idea.* Patrick Benson lives in England.